First published in the United States, Canada, Great Britain, Australia, and New Zealand
in 1995 by North-South Books, an imprint of Nord-Süd Verlag AG, Gossau Zurich, Switzerland.

Copyright © 1992 by Michael Neugebauer Verlag AG
First published in Switzerland under the title
CHRISTIAN MORGENSTERN: KINDERGEDICHTE & GALGENLIEDER
by Michael Neugebauer Verlag AG, Gossau Zurich, Switzerland.

Distributed in the United States by North-South Books Inc., New York

Library of Congress Cataloging-in-Publication Data is available
A CIP catalogue record for this book is available from The British Library
ISBN 1-55858-364-5 (trade binding)   ISBN 1-55858-365-3 (library binding)
TB 10 9 8 7 6 5 4 3 2 1   LB 10 9 8 7 6 5 4 3 2 1   Printed in Hong Kong

CHRISTIAN MORGENSTERN

LULLABIES, LYRICS AND GALLOWS SONGS
SELECTED AND ILLUSTRATED BY LISBETH ZWERGER
TRANSLATED BY ANTHEA BELL

LULLABIES & LYRICS

A MICHAEL NEUGEBAUER BOOK
NORTH-SOUTH BOOKS / NEW YORK / LONDON

LITTLE BELLA

Here is pretty little Bella
Opening her green umbrella.

Opening her green umbrella,
Because it looks like rain, I tell her.

Because it looks like rain, I tell her,
Off you run now, little Bella!

Off you run now, little one,
Off to buy a piece of sun.

To buy a piece of sun, you say:
Hello, good day! Hello, good day!

Hello, good day there, Mr. Bunn!
I want to buy a piece of sun.

I want to buy a piece of sun,
And then the rain will all be done.

And then the rain will all be done.
So back inside goes Mr. Bunn.

And he will give you, for your money,
A piece of sun like yellow honey.

A piece of sun like yellow honey,
Golden honey, sweet and runny,

Like golden honey from the bee,
And he will pack it up for free.

And he will pack it up for free,
So you can bring it home to me.

And when you're home we'll take it out.
Look, a piece of sun, we'll shout!

Half the sun's for little Bella
Half is for the green umbrella.

So off you go now, little one,
Off to buy a piece of sun.

THE BIG ELEPHANT

Here is the king of elephants.
He is the uncle of those aunts.
This elephant of great renown
is pacing, pacing up and down.

The elephant is writing neat
letters to you with his feet,
loving letters in the sand:
Greetings, Sophie Cherryland!

But mind you do not laugh out loud.
The elephant, though huge and proud,
writes less than any other mammal—
much less, for instance, than the camel.

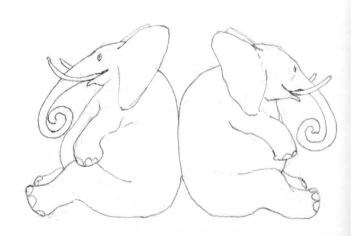

THE SCARECROW

The ravens croaked: Caw, caw, caw, caw!
Who's that we saw? Who's that we saw?
We're not afraid, we're not afraid
of such a silly masquerade!

We know, the ravens said, and smiled,
you're neither woman, man, nor child.
You can't move off and walk away.
In wind and weather there you stay.

You're just two sticks, a coat, a hat.
You think we are afraid of that?
So caw, caw, caw!

THE THREE SPARROWS

Three little sparrows huddled close together,
on a bare nut tree in wintry weather.

One called Donald, one called Dean,
and little Johnny in between.

They keep their eyes closed, one and all,
for soon the snow will start to fall.

Huddling still closer in the storm,
Johnny at least is keeping warm.

Three little hearts, beating with a will—
and if they're not gone,
then they're sitting there still.

FOREST TALE

A giant in the forest strolls;
he has a monstrous ear,
so vast that when the thunder rolls
it only tickles there.

He flicks a careless hand
as if to swat a bumble
bee, and his gentle grumble
shakes the entire land.

On rainy days he falls asleep
and lets his ear become
a lake both wide and deep
where country shepherds come

to water flocks of sheep,
but sometimes, sad to say,
the giant, turning in his sleep,
tips lake and flocks and all away.

GUY

The uncle of a dog called Guy
gave him a very handsome tie
of silk in red and yellow.

His aunt had given him a bell
to tie around his neck as well–
he was a lucky fellow!

He soon grew arrogant and proud,
a fact observed by all the crowd
of dogs he used to meet.

Once Guy would nod a friendly head
or wag his tail, but now instead
he snubs them in the street.

MR. SPOON AND MRS. FORK

Mr. Spoon and Mrs. Fork,
they argued a great deal.
Said Mr. Spoon to Mrs. Fork,
"However big you like to talk,
you're only made of stainless steel!"

Said Mrs. Fork to Mr. Spoon,
"You're as crazy as a loon.
Your face is merely made of tin!
A single, tiny little scratch
would show the world that you're no match
for me–my prongs would win!"

The knife just lay there, having fun.
"Well said," he told the fork. "Well done!"
The spoon regretted what he'd said.
Better to pick no bones, he knew,
with steely people like those two.
He kissed the lady's hand instead!

DREAM SONG   Dream, little one, dream:
                  two trees by a garden stream.

                  One of the trees bears a rose;
                  on the other an apricot grows!

                  A king walks through the garden green
                  and plucks the rose to give his queen.

                  Rose at her breast, she reaches out
                  and picks her king an apricot.

                  The king then breaks the fruit apart
                  and gives her half back, with his heart.

                  They eat the apricot with pleasure,
                  and save its kernel like a treasure.

                  They save the little stone they found
                  inside, and plant it in the ground,

                  wrapped in rose leaves by the queen,
                  the prettiest rose leaves ever seen.

                  Wrapped in rose leaves, safe from harm,
                  tucked in the ground, cosy and warm..

It sleeps there long, it takes its rest
like a bird snug in its nest.

...Dream, little one, dream:
two trees by a garden stream.

One of the trees bears a rose;
on the other an apricot grows!

Dream, little one, dream...

IN WINTER TIME

The lake is freezing over fast;
we'll soon walk on its icy skin.
If a big fish comes swimming past,
he'll bump the ice with nose and fin.
And if I take a little stone
and throw it on the lake, it clitters,
clatters, clitters, clitters, skitters,
flying off, my little stone,
skittering like a bird, it hops,
skimming like a swallow–
till at last my pebble stops
out where we can't follow.
And all the fish will rush in vain
to goggle through the icy pane,
thinking the pebble is something to eat–
but hard as they try to get at the treat,
the ice is too thick, the ice will hold,
they'll simply make their noses cold.

But soon, my dear, just as I told,
soon we can roam that frozen plain
and fetch my pebble back again.

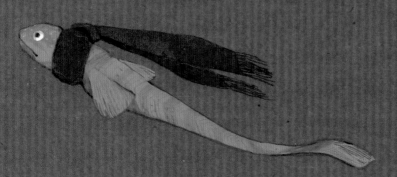

WINTER NIGHT

Once there was a bell—
ding, dong, bell, it rang.
Once a snowflake fell
soft as the bell sang.

Drifting from on high,
down in winter weather,
like an angel's feather
floating in the sky.

Once there was a bell—
ding, dong, bell, it rang.
Once a snowflake fell
soft as the bell sang.

Softly, softly drifting,
thousands fell all night,
until the world was white
as an angel's wing.

Until the world was white
as an angel's wing.

LULLABY

Sleep, my baby, sleep!
Once there was a sheep.

When its fleece was shorn,
the sheep could not keep warm.

A kind man going to the fair
gave the sheep his coat to wear.

Now the sheep is warm and snug,
Wrapped in a coat thick as a rug.

Sleep, my baby, sleep.
Once there was a sheep.

SPRING SONG

Winter, winter, go away,
spring is coming any day!
The ice and snow are going,
the flower buds are showing,
the woods wear green array.

Winter, winter, go away,
hurry now, be on your way!
The little birds are singing,
with joy their throats are ringing
to welcome in the May.

TRANSLATOR'S NOTE

Translating nonsense verse is a fascinating challenge, especially when the verse is by such a poet as Christian Morgenstern, whose work springs from the very heart of the German lyrical tradition. Morgenstern has sometimes been described as the German Edward Lear, but in the variety of style and material his work displays, I think he is more like Lewis Carroll. For instance, just as Lewis Carroll's verse about the "aged, aged, man a-sitting on a gate" suggests Wordsworth's "Resolution and Independence," Morgenstern's "The Worm's Confession" evokes the style of the great nineteenth-century German poet Heinrich Heine. And just as we sense that Carroll's "Jabberwocky" has a meaning deep inside it, for all its nonsense words, the verse that I have translated as "Gruesong" calls up fantastic images, here brought to delicate visual life by Lisbeth Zwerger. In the final resort, however, Morgenstern is like no other poet; he is himself, and unique.

Two of the poems in this book present a translator with no problems, as readers will easily see from a glance at "Fish's Night Song" and "The Big Laloola." The first is an early example of concrete poetry, and still one of the most attractive specimens of the genre; the second is pure sound, described by Morgenstern himself as a "phonetic rhapsody," and in this it differs from "Gruesong," which has its nonsense words linked into a proper grammatical sentence in the original, a sentence I have reflected in the translation. All the other verses in this selection, however, entail special translation problems of their own. Where there are fantastic, invented names for imaginary animals, months, etc., I have used an English equivalent rather than an actual translation, and where a poem hinges on a pun in German (as in "The Prayer," which uses a pun on the German word acht, "eight," and the phrase hab acht, "take care") I have substituted a different pun in translation. I have retained Morgenstern's rhyme schemes, and as far as possible I have also kept his meter, along with its occasional irregularities. Most important of all, I have hoped to suggest his own echoes of such traditional forms as folk song, nursery rhyme, and lyric poetry.

Anthea Bell

GALLOWS SONGS

THE BIG LALOOLA

Kroklokwoffzie? Seemimeemi!
Siyokronto–prufliplo:
Biftsi baftsi; hulaleemi:
quasti basti bo . . .
Laloo laloo laloo laloola!

Hontrarooroo miromenty
zaskoo zes roo roo?
Entypenty, liyolenty
cleckwapuffsie lue?
Laloo laloo laloo laloola!

Simarar kos maltsipempoo
siltsoozankunkrie(;)!
Marjomar dos: Quempoo Lempoo
Siri Suri Si[] !
Laloo laloo laloo laloola!

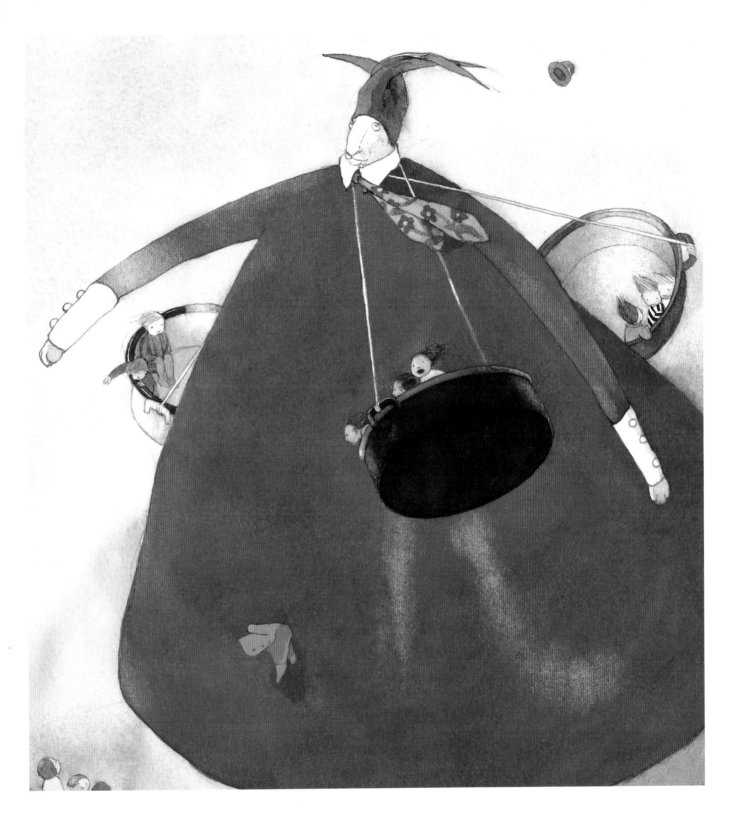

THE FENCE

THERE WAS A FENCE WITH SPACE BETWEEN
THE PLANKS, SO YOU COULD SEE RIGHT IN.

AN ARCHITECT CAME BY ONE DAY
AND STOLE THOSE SPACES ALL AWAY.

HE TOOK THEM TO A BUILDING SITE
TO BUILD A HOUSE TWO FLOORS IN HEIGHT.

THE FENCE WAS LEFT THERE WILLY-NILLY:
A FENCE WITHOUT A SPACE LOOKS SILLY.

IT WAS AN EYESORE IN THE LAND.
THE STATE CONDEMNED IT OUT OF HAND.

AS FOR THE THIEF, HE GOT AWAY
TO AFRIC- OR AMERICAY!

 # A SNAIL TALKS TO ITSELF

Might as well be out of my shell,
Out of my shell might not be as well?
Little way out?
Howabout
inandout
roundabout
woundabout
layabouthereabout
whereabout thereabout…

(Here the snail gets so entangled in its own thoughts, or rather its own thoughts run away with it so much, that it has to put off further consideration of the question to a later date.)

THE WORM'S CONFESSION

A WORM WHO LIVES INSIDE A SHELL
TO ME DID ONCE IMPART,
IN SOFTLY WHISPERED WORDS DID TELL,
THE SECRETS OF HIS HEART.

HE WROTE HIS LOVE A LETTER:
"MY BROKEN HEART PRAY CURE!"
YOU THINK THAT I AM JOKING?
AH, DO NOT BE SO SURE!

A WORM WHO LIVES INSIDE A SHELL
TO ME DID ONCE IMPART,
IN SOFTLY WHISPERED WORDS DID TELL,
THE SECRETS OF HIS HEART.

THE TWO DONKEYS

A dismal donkey, tired of life
said to his lawful wedded wife:

*"We are so stupid, you and I,
why don't we just go off and die?"*

But habit dies hard, as folk say,
and they are living to this day.

IN ANIMAL COSTUME

Palmstrom likes to imitate the animals
and keeps two young tailors busy
making nothing but animal costumes.

He loves to perch like a raven
on the very top branch of an oak tree,
watching the clouds sail by.

Or he likes to be a Saint Bernard,
shaggy head asleep on brave paws,
dreaming of people rescued from the snow.

Or he spins a string net in his garden,
dresses up, and sits all day
like a spider in its web.

Or he swims, a goggle-eyed carp,
around his fountain in his pool
and lets the children feed him.

Or he dangles in stork costume
from the basket of a balloon
and flies away to Egypt.

M FOR EM

All sea gulls look, up in the sky,
as if their names were Em.
With feathers white and soft they fly;
with bird shot you can shoot them.

I've never shot a sea gull dead;
I'd rather let them live.
I feed the gulls on brown rye bread,
and raisins, too, I give.

We humans never can fly free
like sea gulls in the air,
so if your name is Em, then be
glad that you're like them there.

THE COLD

A cold was lurking in the grass,
waiting for some poor soul to pass,

and very soon, with furious rage,
it seized upon a man called Page.

"Ah-choo!" Paul Page caught cold on Monday;
he could not shake it off till Sunday.

Sambucus
LM. Ⅵ glob.

Nux vomica
C.200 glob.

Cepa C.30.
glob.

SONG OF THE GALLOWS BIRDS

How strange is life! How full of dread!

Here we all dangle from red thread.

Toad croaks and spider spins her lair,

the wind blows slantwise through our hair.

O horror, horror, horror howl!

"You are accursed!" cries the owl.

The starlight's broken by the moon,

but you will not be broken soon.

Oh horror, horror, horror cry!

The silver horses gallop by,

the owl hoots twice: tu-whit, tu-whoo!

It chews and brews and blues for you!

GRUESONG

The Flidderfloppet gloameth

through igglywangled wole.

The great red Fangyre boameth,

and ghastly greeks the Grole.

A GALLOWS CHILD'S CALENDAR

Jaguary
Zebruary
Moose
Apeman
Margay
Coon
Shoofly
Aurochs
Sepiabear
Overbear
Novabear
Dinobear

LULLABY OF THE GALLOWS CHILD

Sleep, little one, sleep.
Up in the sky there's a sheep.
A sheep of mist and cloud alive,
like you it struggles to survive.
Sleep, little one, sleep.

Sleep, little one, sleep.
The sun is eating the sheep.
Licking it out of the clear blue air,
with a long, long tongue like a greedy bear.
Sleep, little one, sleep.

Sleep, little one, sleep.
That was the end of the sheep.
The moon comes out and scolds the sun
for eating the sheep–now see him run!
Sleep, little one, sleep.

SUGGESTIONS TO NATURE FOR NEW SPECIES

the **O**xsparrow

the **C**hameleoduck

the **L**ionworm

the **T**oadle

the **L**apowl

the **W**halebird

the **J**ellybug

the **A**rmabullo

the **P**eachuck

the **W**erefox

the **D**ayingale

the **S**ticklefront

the **F**reshwater Kipper

the **V**ine Pug

the **P**layhound

the **E**yewig

the **G**iraffehog

the **R**hinocepony

the **S**wangrass

the **H**eadfruit Tree

THE PRAYER

The little deer pray the night air:
take care!
Take care, *we* pray,
of us poor prey,
take time, keep time,
till midnight
CHIME!
The little deer pray the night air:
take care!
They fold their little hooves in prayer,
the little deer.

DREAM OF THE MOONSHEEP

The moonsheep roams wide fields till dawn,
awaiting sheep shears in the morn.
O moonsheep.

The moonsheep nibbles grassy stalks
plucked from the meadow as it walks.
O moonsheep.

The moonsheep dreams, raising its face:
"I am the heart of all dark space."
O moonsheep.

At dawn the moonsheep will be dead,
its fleece all white, the sun all red.
O moonsheep.

FISH'S NIGHT SONG